For my husband, Jai, with love and thanks.

A CIP catalogue record for this book is available from the British Library.

ISBN 0–7136–3101–5

© 1989 A&C Black (Publishers) Limited

Published by A&C Black (Publishers) Ltd
35 Bedford Row, London WC1R 4JH

Acknowledgements
The author and publisher would like to thank the teachers and pupils of
Northbury Infants' School; also Mrs Bull, Mr Dandy, Ms Seed, Mrs
DeZoysa, Ms Brown, Mr Watt and the Braintree Chinese Restaurant.

Filmset by August Filmsetting, Haydock, St Helens
Printed in Belgium by Henri Proost & Cie Pvba

Stir-fry

Renu Nagrath Woodbridge
Photographs by Jenny Matthews

A&C Black · London

When you're hungry, the dinner queue seems very long. Rachel and Danny are deciding what to eat.

'Chicken-burgers and chips, please,' says Danny.

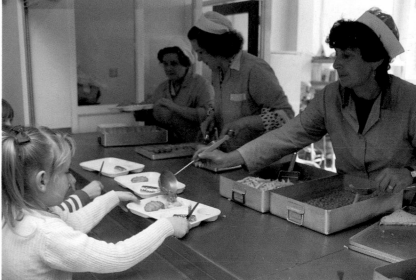

Rachel is having vegetable-rissoles, chips and baked beans. She doesn't eat meat.

3

'Isn't it boring just eating vegetables?'
says Danny.

'Don't you like vegetables, Danny?'
asks their teacher, Mrs Simmonds.

Danny likes potatoes, especially chips.

Do you like potatoes? Here are some different dishes which are made from potatoes.
How many have you tasted?

latkes

potato salad

potato crisps

samosas

baked potatoes

paper dosa

Before they go home, Mrs Simmonds asks all the children to bring in one vegetable for cooking the next day. They are going to cook a vegetable stir-fry.

'What are you going to bring?' Rachel asks her friend Sui Ling. But Sui Ling won't tell. It's a secret.

Rachel's grandad has a greengrocer's shop. He gives her a piece of pumpkin to take to school.

Can you see what her friends have brought?

7

Mohanjit brings some dried lentils from his mum's kitchen cupboard.

Toni asks her mum if she can dig up some potatoes from the garden.

Kevin brings some frozen peas.

Lakhvir picks a fresh cucumber from her mum's greenhouse.

Nobody can guess what Sui Ling
has brought. She gives it to
Mrs Simmonds to keep safely.

'All these vegetables would make
a giant stir-fry,' says Danny.

Do you know the names of all the
vegetables in this picture? You can
find them at the back of the book.

Before the cooking can begin, they have to wash and prepare the vegetables. Daniel is good at this. He helps his mum and dad at home.

Danny and Imran are chopping the courgettes.

Jatinder chops the red peppers and
Rachel cuts off the carrot tops.

Michelle wants to save the carrot tops and
grow them. Can you see how she is doing this?

One of the onions has already started growing,
so Michelle is going to plant it in some earth
to see what happens.

All vegetables are parts of plants.
They are the parts which you can eat.

Some grow underground, like roots and tubers . . .

. . . and bulbs.

Have you ever seen any of these plants growing?

Do you know what they look like above the ground?

These vegetables all grow above the ground.

These are the shoots and stalks of plants . . .

. . . and the leaves.

These are
the seeds
of plants . . .

. . . and the buds.

These are the young flowers . . .

cauliflower

broccoli

. . . and the fruits.

cucumber

red pepper

tomato

green pepper

cucumber

Rachel's class is nearly ready to start cooking. Mohanjit has cut up the broccoli because that's his favourite.

Nibbles, the gerbil, likes broccoli, too.

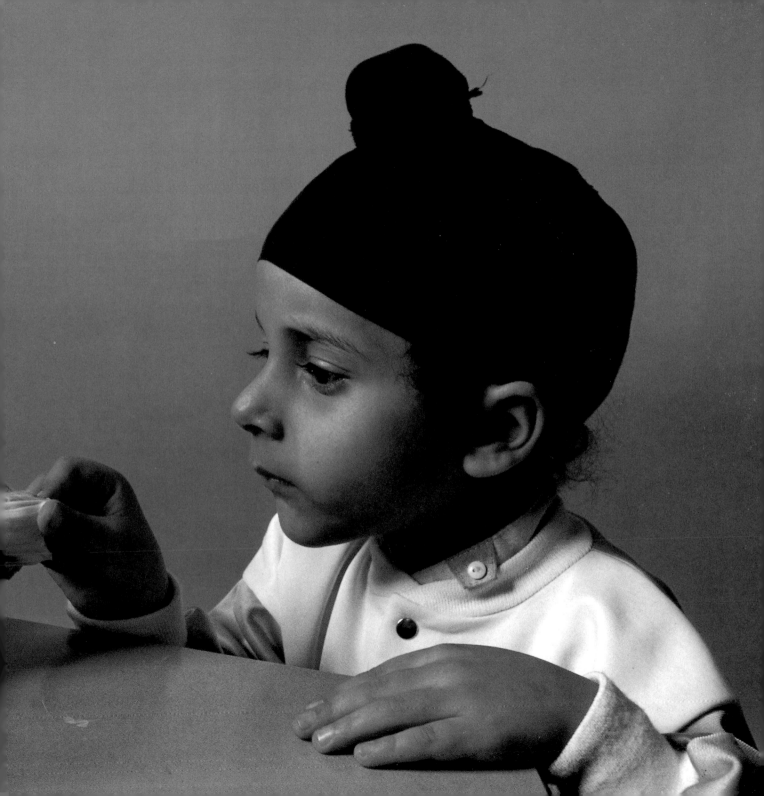

Danny opens a tin of water chestnuts while Tony holds it steady. Can you think why some vegetables are tinned?

'Let's cook the bean sprouts, too,' says Danny. 'They've grown really quickly and the jar is nearly full.'

Mrs Simmonds fries the vegetables. She puts them in one by one because some take longer to cook than others.

At last it's time to open Sui Ling's parcel. What do you think will be inside?

How beautiful!
It's a carrot which has been carved into a dragon.

'Can I have some?' asks Danny.
Doesn't it look good?

24

Things to do

1. This key shows the names of all the vegetables in the photograph on pages 10/11. Can you guess which parts of the plants they come from?

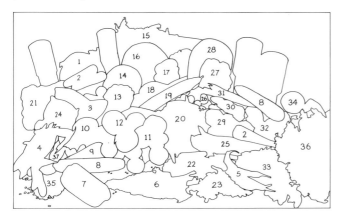

2. Look at the colour, shape and size of a vegetable. Feel it. Is it smooth or rough? How heavy is it? Cut your vegetable in half. Which way do you need to cut it so that one side is the mirror image of the other?

3. Make your own book of vegetables. Cut some vegetables and use them for printing on the cover. In your book you could put:
a) A bar chart of your class's favourite vegetables.
b) Some recipes for savoury and sweet vegetable dishes. Here are a few that you could try: carrot cake; cucumber raita; dal; bortsch; Mexican beans; sweet potato bake and humous.

4. Grow your own vegetables. Have you tried growing mung beans in a jar? Try growing them in two jars; leave one jar in the dark. What do you notice?

5. Find out where most of your vegetables come from. A good trick is to look at the cardboard boxes in the greengrocer's or the market. Look on tins and packets in the supermarket, to find out where frozen and canned vegetables come from.

6. Did you know that some dyes, starch and oils are made from vegetables? Look at packets and boxes in the supermarket to see if they contain vegetable products.

7. Do you know any stories about vegetables? Here are a few for you to look out for: Jack and the Beanstalk; The Great Big Enormous Turnip; The Radish Thief.

1. curly cabbage
2. carrots
3. sweet potatoes
4. mange-tout
5. chillies
6. lentils
7. red pepper
8. courgettes
9. parsnip
10. tomatoes
11. mushrooms
12. onions
13. globe artichoke
14. white cabbage
15. celery
16. red cabbage
17. green pepper
18. potatoes
19. cucumber
20. okra
21. broccoli
22. baby corn
23. kidney beans
24. peas
25. asparagus
26. radishes
27. cauliflower
28. pumpkin
29. garlic
30. ginger
31. runner beans
32. tarot
33. bean sprouts
34. aubergines
35. mung beans
36. coriander
37. tindola